I0536994

FLOWERS FOR HIS LADY

ALINA K. FIELD

HAVENLOCK PRESS

Flowers for His Lady

By Alina K. Field

©2022 Mary J. Kozlowski

ISBN: 9781944063467

Havenlock Press

PO Box 1891

La Mirada, CA 90637

June 25, 2023

Cover design by Mandy Koehler, images by Period Images

Previously published in *Belles & Beaux, a Bluestocking Belles Collection*

Shamed into spinsterhood by a fall from grace years earlier, Eleanor Gurnwood has found a home for herself in the tiny village of Upper Upton, and a quirky, sometimes annoying family in the villagers she's been serving as her vicar-brother's minion. Now, with his rising career, she's faced with a choice: succumb to his pressure to keep house for him elsewhere or stay on in genteel poverty with her new "family".

For now, she has only one goal in sight: to make this year's Christmas service beautiful for the parishioners of St. Tancred's—until the Christmas eve when a man from her past rides in on a white horse.

Major Sir Bramwell Huxley, late of his Majesty's 95th Foot, has ventured on one last mission, a quest for a Christmas miracle: finding the lady he abandoned before leaving for Waterloo. With the help of the villagers of Upper Upton and a bit of Christmas magic, can Bramwell convince Eleanor to take a chance on love again?

Flowers for his Lady is a heartwarming tale of redemption, forgiveness, and the power of love to heal even the deepest wounds.

Previously published in the *Bluestocking Belles Christmas Collection*, 2022.

CHAPTER ONE

23 DECEMBER, 1820

*T*he helpers had departed St. Tancred's hours ago when the wet snow falling showed a determination to stick, as the last few December snowfalls had not done. Besides, some of the members of the Ladies' Society for the Improvement of Village Life had meals to prepare. Those with servants had children to tend to and husbands who would worry about their safe arrival.

Even the new curate, Mr. Godwin, had left, polite and pleased, after a cursory visit in the late afternoon. *He and his wife—a lovely woman due to give birth soon— would serve the people of Upper Upton far better than...*

With a steadying breath, Miss Eleanor Gurnwood shook off what would be an uncharitable thought.

She had stayed on in the peaceful solitude to finish arranging great urns of winter greens and holly, despairing of their broken organ, and the promised flowers from the Brockton Manor greenhouse.

Never mind. This would be a lovely Christmas at St. Tancred's, or at least better than last year's celebration when her brother's cheeseparing meddling had decimated the ranks of her helpful ladies.

He'd left weeks ago, and the ladies had come back.

No one waited at home for her but Millie, her landlord, Galt Wyman's housekeeper. Millie would be ready with her usual meat pie and cabbage mash keeping warm near the hearth. And despite that it was the sabbath, old Galt would be at the Royal George, himself pie-eyed, and cabbage-mashed after too many pints.

The stained glass of the windows, depicting the medieval martyrdom of St. Tancred and his siblings obscured the view, but outside, the winter night glowed with the sort of soft light that comes with a snowfall. She hoped the weather wouldn't spoil the plans for tomorrow night's Christmas Eve Carol service, or the Christmas morning liturgy, or the children's party Christmas afternoon at the Longview Children's Home.

She bent close to the lantern and reached for her watch, remembered she'd sold it to get through the quarter, and sighed. Next year her small trust would be her own to manage and draw from.

The remaining lit candle told her it was likely past seven. Well then, she'd best go rescue Galt before he stumbled his way to the church to fetch *her*. But first…

Three layers of skirts cushioned her knees against

the cold marble as she bent her head and gripped her gloved hands together. *Lord, give me wisdom, guide my path; for pity's sake, send an angel, send someone, to show me the way.*

Tears sprang and she blinked them back. *And cleanse me of this nauseating self-pity.*

It was, after all, her own fault. She'd loved impetuously, with the natural consequence of losing emphatically.

And she wouldn't trade that one experience of love —of loving—for all the rubies in India. Pity herself, she might, and battle the hurt that had followed, but it seemed St. Paul was right—for the love had never quite gone away.

Besides, she wasn't entirely alone. There were good people here in the village of Upper Upton. Her landlord, for one, and his housekeeper. And the innkeeper and his wife. And the matrons and teachers and the young residents of the nearby Longview Children's Home.

She had friends, though those ties were still tenuous. She had hopes of a position at Longview. She also had her brother, who loved her in his own overbearing way.

If only he could display more *charity.*

What really was so terrible about what she'd done? It had been reckless, and foolish, and so wonderful that she pulled out the memory sometimes and savored it. She, destined to spinsterhood, had been loved.

In the end, she'd suffered no more than a wound to her heart and endless hours of tiresome lectures. She felt certain that God had forgiven her. So why did his servant, Reverend Matthew Gurnwood, keep reminding her of that one lapse from propriety?

A man's rumbling voice and the creaking of door hinges accompanied a blast of cold air that blew out the candle's flame.

Blasted Galt. "Please close the door and spare me a moment," she called over her shoulder, "and I'll add a prayer that God in his goodness may spare you the consequences of tonight's imbibing."

"I fear more than a prayer is needed for this fellow, madam."

A frisson of awareness shivered up her spine. The deep, gruff voice caressing her wasn't Galt's. Or Matthew's. Or Mr. Godwin's. And it was no angel's voice.

Memories flooded her with yearning—hopeless yearning for something her pride would balk at receiving. It wasn't him. It couldn't be him.

"Courage," she muttered.

Another blast of cold air swirled around her. She scrambled to her feet, snatched up her heavy mantle and the lantern, and hurried down the aisle.

* * *

WELL AT LEAST THE OLD MAN HE'D UNEARTHED FROM the snow was, apparently, no vagrant.

Major Sir Bramwell Huxley steadied the wispy-haired fellow, a hand clamped to each wiry shoulder while the only light approached like a bobbing specter.

It was dark as the Paris catacombs and just as cold in the church. He'd found the drunken sot sprawled in the lane and half carried him here, the nearest place of refuge.

"I thankee, sir," the fellow croaked in his thick local accent. "Slipped I did, is all. Ellie, you ought to be home. What fool notion is't to hang about here until the snow's as high as a pig's udder."

The shrouded figure arrived, and a feminine scoff came from under the drooping hood. "The same point might be made, Galt, about hanging about too long at the Royal George."

Bram's senses alerted, and he ticked through the incoming facts, sorting them.

That had been no country accent. The fellow was no gentleman, yet he'd called the woman by a first name. He sensed a youngish woman under that heavy wrap, tall and slim. Could she be the fellow's more refined daughter? Or a much younger wife? Surely not a saucy maid, nor the resident vicar's misses. And...

"Would this be the Royal George run by Alexander Grant?" Bram asked.

The woman visibly stiffened.

"The very one," the man said. "And a fine ale he serves too. 'S'not but a few paces from here. Let me buy you a pint fer yer troubles."

"Be off with you both then and make sure the church door is shut." The woman slid around them, her skirts brushing his leg, and a faint scent of lilacs raised the hair on the back of his neck.

Ellie. Could she be Eleanor? *His* Eleanor?

"I'll let Millie know you'll sleep at the inn, Galt," she called over her shoulder.

"Can't do that," the old man said. "Lest I make a bench me bed. Full up, he is. Folks heading to a house party at Lord Cathmore's stopped for the snow."

Lord Cathmore's party had been Bram's excuse for dodging a gathering of distant relatives and traveling to Sussex at Christmas. His excuse, but not his true reason.

"Why, we'll bring him home with us," the old man said. "Why not? Took you in, didn't I, Ellie? Got an extra bed. Room for the horse out back too." He straightened, the charitable impulse seeming to sober him, and turned for the door.

With a sigh, the woman dipped her chin, the heavy hood shielding her face. If he could just get a peek. He followed them out, his fingers itching to yank back the wool and have a glimpse.

Tied to an iron fence rail, his horse shuddered and sent him a baleful look.

"Fine feller he be," the old man said, and Bram chuckled, wondering if he meant the horse or himself.

"On my honor, I'll do you no harm," Bram said, "and since the inn's full, I'll take you up on the offer of hospitality. Allow me." He set his hand over the lady's where she was holding the door pull.

A current shot through him and she snatched her hand away as if she'd been burned as well. She glanced up, mouth agape and quickly turned away.

That moment's shadowed glance made him certain

—almost—and he barely managed a breath to ask, "Shall we lock it?"

She shook her head. "The curate will see to it later."

He pulled the heavy door shut and followed her. Quick stepping was his Eleanor, despite the wet snow swirling around her plenteous skirts. She'd not been dressed so abundantly the last time they met.

Memories of that night stirred him, and in a few long strides he outpaced her and reached the horse. The old man was already there, stroking the white nose.

"Let me put you up on my horse, Miss, er..."

* * *

HE WANTED AN INTRODUCTION, DID HE?

"Take my arm, Galt," she said. "You, sir, may mount and follow us."

"I most certainly will not ride while a lady walks." He cupped his hands. "And if you won't ride, miss, well, up you go, Mr. Galt."

Tugging her wrap tighter, she trudged on, eyes on the treacherous path ahead. That one glimpse, dark though it was, had revealed an iron jaw formed by generations of breeding, the hook of a powerful nose, and lips that could soften in the sweetest of kisses.

Swallowing a rising heat, she sensed him joining her, the reins swallowed up in one of his gloved hands. The heat of his big body swept through her, and his scent washed over her, a mixture of horse, his particular shaving soap, and the indefinable and not unpleasant musk that was his alone.

He was flesh and blood and all male. What was she to *do*?

She straightened her spine. The past was the past. He with his white horse was no knight come to seek her out. The promises he'd made—the promises they'd both made—had gone awry. Matthew had interfered, no doubt, but so had the Crown, and she couldn't begrudge a man who'd sworn his service there. It wasn't that he hadn't cared for her, but that duty had called more strongly.

He'd gone away, and now he was passing through the village. He hadn't come seeking *her*… yet, here they were, and the air around them all but vibrated with his curiosity.

She would face this squarely, head-on, with her dignity intact. "Yes," she said quietly, "It is I."

His free hand sought hers and, flummoxed again, she allowed it to be captured, holding her breath for an apology or explanation or—God help her—a sweet word. Or something.

And he said nothing.

MILLIE GREETED THEM AT THE BACK DOOR OF THE cottage, her dark eyes flashing fire. "Mind my clean floor. And who've you brought home this time, Galt Wyman. Who is this fellow, Ellie?"

A bounder of gigantic proportions, she wanted to say, but Galt spoke first.

8

"Picked me up out of the snow, he did, old woman, and a woman with eyes in her head can see he's quality. Lay the table for one more. And the bed in the spare room. Clean sheets. Come through, sir, come through," he said, beckoning.

Eleanor stepped into the room and pushed back her hood. She fixed her gaze on the visitor and felt the heat of his hazel eyes. His light brown hair needed a trim, and the sight of his bristly whiskers, a shade darker, sent a shiver through her, remembering...

Swallowing a surge of lust, she steadied herself. "Perhaps introductions first, Galt?"

* * *

DARK HAIR SPILLED OUT OVER ELEANOR'S FOREHEAD AND cheeks, making her look like the fresh young lass barely out of the schoolroom he'd met almost six years ago. Though, he supposed she hadn't been so young then. She'd only looked it. She must be six-and-twenty now, or perhaps seven-and-twenty. She was thinner, and something had happened besides his desertion, something to leave the dent of too many frowns between her beautiful dark winged eyebrows.

She cleared her throat, and he realized he was gaping back at her, tongue-tied.

"I am indeed a boarder here," she said. "Our host is Mr. Galt Wyman, and this is his housekeeper, Mrs. Millie Chatworth."

"Pleased to meet you," he said, finding his voice. "I am Bramwell Huxley."

9

Eleanor cocked her head. "*Major* Bramwell Huxley?"

He nodded. "On half-pay for now." And how the devil did she know about his promotion?

She raised an eyebrow. "Major *Sir* Bramwell Huxley?"

Blasted Alexander Grant must have been talking. He dipped his head.

"Why, you two know each other?" the housekeeper said. "Yer acquainted with our Miss Gurnwood?"

"And not to let on to me, Ellie," Galt said. "For shame, girl."

Anger flashed across her face, and he remembered her brother. The good reverend had called out her innocent friendliness more than once at that long ago house party. He could only imagine how he'd addressed the less than innocent behavior. If he'd learned of it.

He must have. Gurnwood had made sure there'd be no further connection between his sister and a lowly captain.

"The merest acquaintance," Eleanor said, "years ago."

It wasn't a mere acquaintance, dammit. It had been a heart-swelling affair with a soul-rattling ending, followed by war.

"Five years and nine months to be precise," he said. "And there is nothing for Miss Gurnwood to be ashamed of."

The shame was all his.

Eleanor shed her cloak, a heavy shawl, her gloves, and a bonnet, and he couldn't look away.

"Sir Bramwell is more a friend of my brother," she said.

He bristled with a flash of anger. Matthew Gurnwood, the pompous hypocrite of a clergyman had never been his friend. He'd known him, briefly, at Oxford, before leaving to go into the army.

Why hadn't Gurnwood taken her in? Why was she forced to take a room with good-hearted yokels? "And where is your brother now?"

"In Chichester," she said.

"Aye," Galt said. "Promoted to sub-dean."

The housekeeper bustled about, setting a kettle to the fire. "He'll be back Christmas day, Ellie says."

"And there'd best be room at the inn for him," Galt said, "because he's not staying here."

The housekeeper clucked. "I suppose he'll go to the vicarage and push Mr. Godwin and his wife out of their bed, and her with a babe coming so soon."

Well, well; Reverend Matthew Gurnwood wasn't well liked by the locals either.

"What of the flowers?" the housekeeper asked. "Did her ladyship send them?"

"Flowers?" he asked. "In winter?"

"For the altar," the housekeeper said. "To add to the greenery. Our Ellie is always scrounging about to see the altar properly dressed, isn't that so? And her ladyship has a greenhouse with blooms all year round, isn't that right, Ellie? St. Tancred's had a small greenhouse until last year's storms and Mr. Gurnwood wouldn't make repairs."

"Your brother was vicar here?" he asked, more by

11

way of confirming something he'd already heard. "For how long?"

"Too long," Galt muttered, and Eleanor sent the old man a quelling look.

She went to a cabinet and came back with a bottle and two glasses. "We came to St. Tancred's a little more than a year ago. And Millie, you well know the money was needed for repairs to the church roof. Come along, Galt. Why are you standing around here in your kitchen when you have a perfectly fine dining room?"

* * *

IT WAS ELEANOR HERSELF WHO LED HIM TO THE SMALL bedchamber under the eaves after his host had passed out midsentence in his small parlor.

Over dinner, Bram had done his best to answer Galt's many questions providing as little information as possible without outright lying.

Why was he here? To attend the party at Brockton Hall.

How did he know Lord Cathmore? They'd served together at Waterloo.

And the subject of Waterloo had pulled a shade down over the old man's face. Eleanor declared she knew Galt had questions and would leave them to talk.

Galt had lost a grandson at Waterloo and begged to know what had happened there.

By necessity, they'd polished off one bottle of surprisingly good brandy and opened another, helping him wade through those blood-soaked memories, helping him parse his words. Galt didn't need to know the full horror of what the lad might have endured.

He was clutching an empty glass and his host was snoring when Eleanor entered, threw a shawl over Galt, and beckoned him. He went readily. Following her was what he'd wanted to do the entire evening.

His shelter for the night might have once been a servant's room, sparsely furnished with a narrow bed, a plain deal bureau, and a washstand. It smelled of soap, clean linen and wood smoke. He turned the bedside oil lamp higher. The bedding looked fresh, and a fire burned brightly in the small unadorned hearth.

While he and Galt drowned bad memories, Eleanor had prepared this room for him.

His heart lifted. The coldness she'd displayed this night was a false front. She was still the kindest girl he'd ever met, though she was no longer a girl. She was a woman, the woman for him.

When he turned back to thank her, she had already departed.

He hurried down the corridor after her and knocked at the door she'd just closed.

CHAPTER TWO

"Do you need something?" she called through the closed door. Not *Go away*.

His confidence soared and he tried the knob—it was unlocked—and stepped in.

Eleanor's room was only a tad larger than his own, with the same amenities, except that the fireplace was larger and the fire in it smaller. Was color flooding her cheeks? It was hard to see in the dim light, but he hoped it was so. He hoped she felt something.

He wanted her more than he ever had before, but he reminded himself to go slowly.

"What is it, Major? Do you need something?"

He'd caught her in the act of feeding the fire. She'd cast off her heavy shawl, and the coil of hair on the back of her head had loosened, dark tendrils touching her cheeks and shoulder.

The fireplace poker in her hand wobbled.

"Yes, I do need something," he said, and his feet

carried him closer of their own accord. "I need you, Eleanor."

"That is the brandy speaking," she said with a brittleness she'd not shown all those years earlier. "Go to bed."

Gutted. His battlefield experience, his medals, his exploits, meant naught now. He'd given her his heart. They'd made promises, but she hadn't wanted to wait.

She blinked and pressed her lips together on an unmistakable tremor that passed through him as well, and he knew.

He'd hurt her terribly.

ELEANOR HELD HER BREATH, WAITING TO SEE WHAT HE would do next.

What she would do, if he decided to step even nearer.

A shiver passed through him. The room was chilly, but big men like Bram only shivered when they were ill or...

She set aside the poker. "You and Galt spoke of Waterloo."

When the subject came up, she'd seen pain in Galt's face and reluctance in Bram's and had left them to hash it out.

Oh, she'd been curious. She'd wanted to stay. She wanted to know where Bram had been, what he'd experienced. Whether he'd suffered.

But if she did, she'd be tempted to open her heart and be hurt all over again.

He stepped close and lifted her clenched hands, untangling them. "We did." He studied her face, clear-eyed. "I suppose I *am* foxed. And I won't... I won't trouble you tonight. Except to tell you, I've never forgotten you, and we must talk."

He lifted her hands and bestowed a kiss on the back of each one, sending her heart tumbling.

She shook her head. "What is there to say?"

"When I heard Matthew Gurnwood was the vicar here, I had to know what became of you. You're not married. Why didn't you marry? Your brother said—"

"*My brother?*" What exactly had Matthew done?

"You were betrothed to some clergyman fellow."

"I most certainly was *not*." Oh, Matthew had hoped to bring about a match between her and a widowed clergyman with powerful connections in the church hierarchy. Matthew had blamed the failure of the match to her fall from grace at the house party where she'd met Bram, but in truth, if she had to marry an old coot, she'd sooner marry Galt.

"What about you, Bram? Did Lady Felicity finally snare you when you returned to London?" Lady Felicity Spanning, newly widowed, had attended the house party. It was clear to all she'd set her sights on the handsome young military officer who was heir to a baronet.

"Who? No. Of course not. And I only passed through London on my way to Deal."

"But after you left, Lady Felicity told me—"

"No," he said, his mouth firming, his eyes burning

into her. "She was nothing to me. I've only ever thought of you."

Some strong emotion—anguish perhaps—sparked in his eyes, quickly extinguished. His hands firmed around hers, warm and strong. The brash young man she'd fallen for had suffered. He was battle-hardened.

That young man hadn't forced himself on her before; she was certain the man he'd become wouldn't either.

But she'd hardened too, hadn't she? She wouldn't succumb to a man who'd left her with nary a goodbye.

One big hand pulled away and cradled her jaw. "Ah, Eleanor." He swallowed, and his eyes glistened. "Thank you for preparing a comfortable room for me." His lips brushed hers in a featherlight kiss, sending a tingle all the way to her frigid toes.

Hades. She was well on her way to losing her heart again.

He stepped back and bowed. "We'll talk tomorrow," he said, and then slipped out the door.

BRAM AWOKE WITH A START AND LOOKED AROUND, seeking a memory of where he was and how...

Eleanor was here.

And she'd promised to talk. Although, as he threw back the covers and shivered in the chill morning, he recollected that she hadn't made any such promise. He'd been too foxed to try to extort one from her.

So foxed that he'd slept naked, a sure sign that this

house had felt safe. He stirred the embers, fed the fire, and set the bucket of water someone had left to heat.

Someone had also brought up his kit—or maybe it had been here in the dark corner the night before. He quickly shaved, dressed, and made himself as presentable as a man could in wrinkled clothes and without a valet.

The housekeeper greeted him in the kitchen. "S'pose you'll be wanting breakfast after sleeping half the day away."

He glanced out the small window. The overcast sky revealed nothing about the hour.

"It's nigh onto ten of the morn. Go on then into the dining room and I'll fetch you a plate."

He pulled out a chair. "I'll eat here, and I'm grateful for whatever is on offer. Is Miss Gurnwood still about?"

"Went out earlier." She bustled about, the delectable odor of bacon and toast sending him back to his mostly happy childhood. The Huxley cottage had always been filled to the brim with friends and his female cousins from the nearby manor house that was now his. The toast appeared in front of him, along with a tub of butter, a pot of jam, and tea.

"Do you expect her back soon?" he asked.

"Who can tell? Ellie comes and goes as she pleases now that she's out from under..." She chewed her lip. "Now that her brother has left." She set down a plate laden with bacon, sausage, eggs, and beans. "Christopher Godwin called this morning, and Ellie fetched him home to his mama, along with my fresh biscuits."

The enticing smells made his mouth water. "Christopher Godwin?"

"The curate's boy."

"Ah. Did Miss Gurnwood move in here when her brother left?"

"Aye. She couldn't very well stay in the vicarage with Mr. Godwin before his wife and babes arrived. She thought to go and stay at Longview, but the vicar squashed that notion. Didn't hold with Maria and Alex Grant taking her in neither. Wasn't happy about Galt, to be honest, him being a widower, never mind I'm here allus and old Galt has fifty years on her. Now, leave the dishes when you're done and I'm off to tidy up after Galt."

The vicarage, Longview, and the inn had been Eleanor's choices.

"Miss, Millie," he said. "Whose home is Longview?"

"Belongs to Lord Cathmore, and I suppose Lord Hackwell too since both their ladies are patrons. It's a children's home. Filled to the brim with 'em."

"A school?"

The housekeeper snorted. "Orphans, the lot, or as like to be orphans. The vicar didn't hold with his sister mingling with, beg yer pardon for plain-speaking, sir, bastards." She turned back at the door. "She'll most likely look in at the church after the vicarage. Make sure all is ready for tonight."

"Tonight?"

"It's Christmas Eve. There'll be a carol service."

Ah. She'd been in the church decorating. He remembered something about flowers.

"Too much brandy for me last night."

"And too much for Galt. I reckon he's off to the Royal George for some hair of the dog." She nodded. "Straight down the high street. You can't miss it. And it mayen't be my place to ask, but will you be staying on here for Christmas or traveling on?"

He looked down at his almost empty plate. He was expected at Brockton Manor for Christmas. But Eleanor was here until he could pry her away from the village and convince her to....

To what? He now had a manor house, filled as it was with an aunt and cousins. He didn't have the heart to throw them out.

He'd have to ford that river when he came to it and hope his cannon didn't sink and his horse drown. "I'll beg another night of your hospitality, Miss Millie, if I may." She harrumphed and departed.

He took one last bite and carried his empty plate to the sideboard. Some hair of the dog was in order for him as well. One drink, a short chat with Alex Grant, and then he'd seek out Eleanor at the church.

"Do you think Auntie Liv has made scones for Wills?' Christopher Godwin turned up his freckled face and in doing so almost dropped the bundle of biscuits he was bringing his friend.

"Careful, young Chris," Eleanor said, "else you'll be

bringing your friend mud pies instead of ginger biscuits."

A wicked gleam passed through his face, and she laughed. "Give them to me. Millie didn't spend hours baking these for you to drop them. I'll carry them and claim one for my troubles."

He straightened and clutched them closer to his thin breast. His clothes were warm, but ill-fitting. The poor lad was growing fast. When the opportunity for a promotion in Chichester came up, her brother had brought in Mr. Godwin to serve St. Tancred's. Matthew felt magnanimous about allowing the curate and his wife the use of the vicarage, but he really ought to be giving Mr. Godwin a greater share of the tithes.

The Royal George Inn looked busy today with more horses moving in and out of the stables. She waved to Barty, the Longview lad Mr. Grant hired as a groom when he wooed Maria away from her job at Longview and married her.

Grant, Cathmore, and Hackwell had all served together in the army. With Longview nearby, Lords Cathmore and Hackwell wanted a respectable inn for wealthy visitors and potential donors. They'd inveigled Grant, outcast son of a Scots laird, to take up the management of the inn. With his affable hospitality and their patronage, the inn had prospered.

She opened the inn door and felt a rush of warmth from the well-tended fire. It was Christmas Eve, and yet the taproom was busy. Most likely the men were getting out from underfoot of their busy wives. She waved a greeting to Galt, ensconced by the fire with some of his cronies.

Alexander Grant beamed his usual friendly smile. "Happy Christmas, Miss Gurnwood. And Christopher, what have you there?"

"Biscuits," the lad said.

"For me?"

Christopher's face fell. Grant laughed and tousled his hair. "Wills is back in the kitchen bedeviling Aunt Liv. Run ahead. Miss Gurnwood, before you go back to visit with Maria, will you greet my esteemed visitors?"

"Esteemed visitors? Would one of those be Lord Cathmore with my flowers?"

"Miss Gurnwood." Maxwell Hamish, Viscount Cathmore, rose from his chair, and the three other men at his table stood as well.

She recognized Lord Hackwell, who she'd met at the parish's spring assembly. The second man she didn't know, but he was, like the other two lords, tall, handsome, dark-haired, and aristocratic looking.

The third man was Bram.

She felt heat rising into her cheeks. Of course, he knew their lordships. His promotion and news of his baronetcy she'd culled from the newssheets. She might have puzzled out that they'd been in the army together.

She was naught but the vicar's spinster sister, no one of consequence, and grateful for Hackwell and Cathmore's courtesy. Not so grateful for the curious gaze and twitching lips of the man introduced as Lord Ottershaw.

And Bram... best not be grateful for his courtesy.

"We shall expect you at Brockton Manor," Lord Cathmore was saying. "Let me send a carriage for you this afternoon. Last night's snow has melted, and the roads are quite passable."

The invitation had already been extended by Lady Cathmore, and she'd turned it down.

"I thank you for the kindness," she said, "But I fear I have duties at St. Tancred's."

"Surely not," he cried. "Not now that your brother has hired a curate and gone off to Chichester."

"I am helping Mr. and Mrs. Godwin settle in. And speaking of that..." She took in a breath. In for a penny, in for a pound. "Did you perchance bring along the promised flowers from Brockton Manor's hothouse?"

Alex Grant chuckled at Lord Cathmore's puzzlement. Lord Hackwell smiled. Lord Ottershaw's lip curled up in a sneer.

Color was rising in Bram's cheeks, sending a flurry of heat into her own.

He was embarrassed. She swallowed a rising fury.

"Ach, Cathmore," Grant said, "flowers for the church, of course. Maria spoke with your lady about them."

"I am sorry, Miss Gurnwood," Lord Cathmore said. "I didn't know."

"Flowers?" a lady's voice said. "I adore flowers."

Lady Felicity Spanning sailed up to the group, parting the warm congenial air like a roving iceberg. Stiff blond curls peeked from under her bonnet, the red plumes of the elaborate piece died to match the fur-lined mantel draping her willowy figure.

Dressed for travel—thank heavens, she would be leaving soon.

"My dear sister, it seems our host, Cathmore, is also a florist," Lord Ottershaw said.

Lady Felicity tittered, and then caught sight of the sandy-haired man, the tallest one of the group. "Bram," she cried. "My dear brother, you didn't tell me Bram would be attending the party. You are, aren't you?" She sidled over, linked arms with Bram, and mimed a surprised face at Eleanor. "Why, if it isn't Miss Gormhall." She batted her eyes. "Or... surely, you're a Mrs. now?"

Bram's mouth firmed, his color still high. He glanced down at the arm linked with his but didn't try to pull away.

Eleanor dipped her chin a fraction, all that she would offer this haughty...

She took in a breath. "How do you do, Lady Felicity. Merry Christmas, my lords." She spotted Maria entering the taproom holding her daughter and managed a smile for Grant. "And now, I fear I must be off. Good day to you all."

Maria hurried to greet her and pass over baby Elspeth who'd crowed a greeting and put out her arms to the newcomer.

Maria leaned close. "Is aught wrong? I wondered what could be holding you up—oh." She set an arm about Eleanor's shoulder. "That woman," she muttered. "So unpleasant. So unlike Lady Cathmore and Lady Hackwell. I should like to attend the house party just to watch *our* grand ladies deal with her."

Eleanor smiled, and then laughed. "I'm sure they'll deal kindly with her."

"Says the vicar's sister."

She shuddered, feeling herself a fraud. If only Maria knew.

"Has she set her cap for the major?" Maria asked as they entered the kitchen.

Eleanor's heart sank. Felicity had set her cap for the Major five years and nine months ago. Perhaps she was another reason he'd stayed away so long.

A cold knife pierced her heart remembering the words whispered in the night, the kisses, the feel of his big body over hers. The promises. Had Bram done with Felicity what he'd done with Eleanor? Had he made promises there as well?

They entered the kitchen, and she brought her attention away from a sudden surge of anger and grief to greet the chattering boys.

* * *

BRAM WATCHED ELEANOR'S PROUD BACK STIFFEN AS SHE turned away and walked toward Grant's wife and infant. The babe reached for Eleanor who accepted it with delight, and then the ladies put their heads together like bosom friends.

"*She's* not aged well," Lady Felicity said softly. "Poor thing."

Bram scanned the painted face and looked down at the gloved talons wrapping his arm. "We've all aged, Lady Felicity."

She gasped dramatically, pulling her arm away, as he'd hope she would. "*Bram.* That is not a gallant thing to say to a lady."

Cathmore's lips twitched. "You're as lovely as the day we met, Lady Felicity."

"Which was last month in London," she said with a stiff smile. "The carriage is waiting outside, brother. I'm anxious to meet your ladies, my lords. We can all cram in if you like."

"Thank you, but Hackwell and I rode here. We have a call to pay and then we'll be along shortly."

"Certainly, Bram must ride with us," Lady Felicity said. "Oh, say that you will, Bram. Why, I'm sure my brother would be happy to ride outside while I grant you a chance to redeem yourself."

"How generous of you," Bram said. "Cathmore, a word, if you don't mind, before you depart."

Cathmore raised an eyebrow.

"Come along, Felicity," Ottershaw said. "Their lordships will catch up with us apace."

The four men watched them leave.

"One more round, innkeeper," Hackwell said.

Grant laughed, and led them to the bar, pouring a brandy for each of them. "Well, Huxley," he said, "mayhap you'll soon join the ranks of happily married men."

Bram shuddered. "*Happily,* indeed."

"She's certainly made her intentions known," Hackwell said.

Cathmore smiled. "And I'd say Huxley here has made his intentions known as well." He laughed.

"Going to beg off from my house party, are you, and stay here with Grant?"

"Actually," Bram said, "as the inn was full, one of the generous locals took me in last night. I thought I might stay another night and attend tonight's carol service."

"Who took you in?" Grant blinked and then a sly smile spread. "Galt Wyman, was it?" He glanced at the other two men. "Since her brother left, Miss Gurnwood lodges there with old Galt and his housekeeper."

"Well then," Hackwell said, "you may as well attend the Christmas party at Longview tomorrow afternoon."

"The children's home?"

"Yes. Our ladies are patronesses of the establishment. In fact, we are running an errand there right now for our wives."

"Miss Gurnwood is quite involved there as well, now that her stiff-necked brother has departed," Grant said. "His support of Longview was lukewarm at best."

"He kept Eleanor away?" Bram asked, and then he remembered what Millie had said earlier.

Grant grinned. "Eleanor, is it?"

Three pairs of eyes studied him, and blast it, his cheeks began to burn. "I met her and her brother several years ago. In fact, Lady Felicity attended the same house party."

Grant nodded. "Miss Gurnwood—Eleanor—is cut from the same cloth as my Maria and I'd daresay Cathmore's and Hackwell's ladies. Her kindness isn't

27

just put on for Sunday mornings. She's a lady who likes children, no matter how they were birthed."

Bram tossed back his drink and set down the glass, thinking.

A home for orphans, or ones who are like orphans, Millie had said. Why did Eleanor have such a particular interest in the place?

Cold slithered down his back. Had he got her with child all those year ago?

"I'll ride along with you today," he said.

CHAPTER THREE

*E*leanor conveyed Christopher and his bundle of warm scones to the vicarage, then popped into the church to see the previous day's labor in the full light of day.

It was magnificent. Red, white, and gold banners streamed from the foiled star hanging over the large creche. The manger stood empty, ready to be filled when the children brought in the baby Jesus at the end of the service. Lush boughs of pine, box, and juniper filled urns; Holly and mistletoe berries added color. The promised Christmas roses and amaryllis would have topped off the adornments.

Perhaps next year, if she were still here.

Battling a heavy heart, she retraced her steps back to Galt's. Milly stood in the warm kitchen, laboring over more baking. It smelled divine.

"There you be," she said, retrieving the kettle from the grate. "Water's hot. Sit you down and try some of my current cake. Oh, and Galt brought back a letter for you."

She shed her outerwear and let Millie serve her, grimacing at the handwriting on the letter before opening it.

My dear sister,

You will be pleased to know that I've taken a goodly house with well-kept furnishings near the cathedral. You should be able to manage it quite well with a maid or two.

I know that you will be anxious to join me here, and so, I've advanced my plans and will arrive at the Royal George in time for the evening carol service. I've written separately to Grant, and you will remove yourself forthwith from your current abode to the inn, where a room will be waiting.

By another stroke of good fortune, I'm to be accompanied by the Archdeacon, the Venerable Felix Millington. He is recently widowed, and quite eligible, and dare I say, eager to meet you. It would not do for you to be discovered residing unchaperoned in the home of a single man.

Be sure to have your trunk conveyed to the inn as well, as we shall all depart for Chichester after the morning services.

You will, I trust, conduct yourself with the decorum fitting my new assignment.

SHE PUT THE LETTER ASIDE AND STARED INTO HER teacup.

"Bad news?" Millie asked.

She straightened and inwardly shook herself. "It's from my brother. He's arriving tonight instead of tomorrow."

"Hmm," Millie said. "And when does he leave?"

"Tomorrow after the morning services."

Millie took a seat across the table. "He's not staying here."

"He's written to Mr. Grant to take rooms."

"Rooms? As in more than one?"

"Three, actually. He's bringing along the Archdeacon. And he instructs me to remove to the inn for the night so that I can be ready to leave with them in the morning."

Millie made a noise low in her throat. "We're not good enough I suppose."

Eleanor shook her head. "The Archdeacon is recently widowed and quite eligible. And Matthew doesn't want me to be found residing unchaperoned in the home of a single man."

The ridiculousness of it overcame her, and a laugh bubbled up and spilled over.

Millie reached across the table and took her hand. "Don't go," she said. "Stay here the night with us, and longer. Galt won't mind. Although." She grimaced. "I s'pose when your brother discovers the Major here under the same roof, he might have an apoplexy."

"The Major? No, he's off to Brockton Manor for the Cathmores' Yuletide party."

Millie shook her head. "Nay. He told me hisself before he left this morning, he'll be here tonight."

"Well then, he must have changed his mind. I saw him leave the Royal George with Lord Cathmore and some others attending the party."

"He'd best send someone for his kit, then."

31

"I'm sure he will."

And that would be that as far as Bram Huxley was concerned.

"You look peaked," Millie said. "Best go and have a lie down before dinner. I've a beef joint a-roasting."

"Should I not stay and help—"

"Shoo." Millie matched her hands to her words. "With only three mouths and my own to feed, I can manage with one arm tied behind me back."

Three mouths. She shoved down the foolish hope that Millie had the right of it, and Bram would return from Brockton Manor in time for their dinner.

But Galt and Millie kept country hours. Bram would never make it to Brockton Manor and back by dinner.

"You're still here?" Millie asked.

Eleanor managed a laugh and obeyed, climbing the narrow stairs to her room.

* * *

"WHAT ARE YOU SO BLUE-DEVILED ABOUT, HUXLEY?" Hackwell asked.

"I'm not."

"Oh ho. Cathmore, has the Major not been frowning since we left Longview?"

"Indeed, he has. Do you not approve of our wives' charity? Or does the long face have something to do with you seeking out children around the age of five?"

Blast it. Cathmore had overheard his conversation with the matron, the nosy bugger. He spurred his horse into a canter, but Hackwell kept pace with him and called, "Is there aught you wish to tell us about? I've told you my family's scandal, so you know there'll be no judging."

Hackwell had discovered both his own father's and brother's by blows living under the care of the future Lady Hackwell.

He reined up and rubbed his jaw, and the other two men stopped as well.

Perhaps Hackwell's history had unconsciously prodded his worries. But he'd found no children at Longview that fit his suspicions.

"I mentioned that just before Waterloo, I attended a house party in Leicestershire. It was at the home of a school friend. Friends of his from Oxford were in attendance, clerical types, along with others."

"Reverend Gurnwood?" Cathmore asked.

"Just so. Plus, some stuffy cleric he was trying to impress."

"And Miss Gurnwood?"

"Yes."

"Ah."

"I thought you were looking at her rather warmly," Hackwell said. "What happened... no, never mind, if you're looking around Longview for a child of a certain age, I can guess what happened. Did she cast you off?"

Had she? He'd gone off overnight to visit a friend recovering from wounds and returned to find that she and her brother had left. And then the summons had come to report for duty.

He'd sent her a letter, and she'd never replied. He'd

33

sent an emissary in the person of his host and was told his attentions weren't welcome.

That information arrived after the battle, and he'd gone his way to other duties, shipped off to Canada and then the West Indies. The guilt and, dammit, the hurt had flamed back to life when he'd learned that Matthew Gurnwood was vicar in this small village only a few miles from Brockton Manor.

"Well, if you ask me," Cathmore said, "the problem lies with that pompous brother of hers. Never did think much of the fellow, but the living wasn't mine to manage."

"You and Miss Gurnwood." Hackwell laughed, and then sent him a sheepish look. "Sorry, old fellow. Miss Gurnwood seems a good sort of girl. Don't know what she sees in you."

"I rather think she despises me."

"Ah, no, not from what I saw," Cathmore said. "What are you going to do?"

Perhaps it wasn't too late. "I'm going to win her back."

"Hah," Cathmore said. "A woman once spurned," he grimaced, "or a woman who thinks she was spurned, requires a special kind of wooing."

"Cathmore learned this wooing his lady," Hackwell said. "Having also put the cart before the horse."

He recalled Cathmore's story of his temperamental bride.

Miss Gurnwood wasn't temperamental. She was a proud and sensible woman.

He hadn't spurned her, but she was still holding him

at arm's length. Did she care for him? Did he have a chance with her?

"What does she want most in the world?" Cathmore asked.

He reined up and looked around the winter landscape, bleak and barren like the last few years of his life. Had Eleanor experienced the same sort of loneliness?

"You must make a grand gesture," Cathmore said. "It's Christmas after all."

"You must bring her the perfect gift," Hackwell said. "What does she want, man?"

He spotted a holly bush with its red berries. Galt's fireplace mantel had been adorned with them, a bit of color in the drab. But Eleanor wanted more.

"Lead the way to Brockton Manor, Cathmore," he said. "I know just what to bring her."

HEART HEAVY, ELEANOR LEFT RIGHT AFTER DINNER FOR the church. Bram had not appeared, as she'd known he wouldn't. Galt had arrived home well into his cups but had rallied over the excellent roast beef.

Millie had spared Galt her brother's news and commands, and Eleanor had kept mum about them as well. She wouldn't move to the Royal George tonight. All the same, she gave both her host and his housekeeper their Christmas gifts, embroidered handkerchiefs for Galt, and a summer shawl she'd knitted on the sly for Millie.

One never knew what lengths Matthew might go

35

to. He'd whisked her away from the house party all those years ago, not even giving her a chance to wait for Bram's return.

The old hurt chilled her. Matthew had pulled her away, and Bram had not followed her.

Lifting her skirts, she picked her way down the High Street. She'd donned her best winter gown, a red wool with a beaded neckline and flounces, but in view of the muddy streets, she'd donned practical half boots with it. The dress had been a gift from the lady patroness of Matthew's last parish before coming to St. Tancred's. A hand-me-down, but not one that had been worn much. Matthew had frowned at the color and the scooped neckline, but she'd been thrilled both to receive it and to know that he couldn't object without insulting the giver.

She pushed open the church door and was surprised to find two people there already, going about lighting candles.

Mr. Godwin cast her a bright smile. "Ah, here is our savior, my love."

His wife—indeed it was her—waddled down the altar stairs and came to grasp Eleanor's hands. "Dear Miss Gurnwood," she said. "The church looks divine. What would we have done without you?"

"You have an excellent group of parishioners who—"

"Who don't know me at all." She smiled. "Not to mention, the children to see to, including this one." She rubbed her belly. "My dear aunt has arrived just this evening and is taking the little ones in hand and tucking them in. I'll go and fetch Christopher betimes so he can be with his choirmates and friends. By Christmas next year, I'll know all the ladies and even before then I'm sure I'll be able to follow in your excellent footsteps when you leave for Chichester."

Her heart fell even further. She wasn't needed here, at least not in her old role at St. Tancred's. But there was still the chance for a position at Longview to pursue.

She forced a smile. "I'm afraid you won't see the last of me soon. I have no plans to go to Chichester."

Mr. Godwin had joined them, and a troubled look formed on his face. "I received a letter from your brother just this afternoon saying he was taking you away tomorrow."

"Yes. I received a letter with the same message. But I'm determined to attend the party at Longview Manor tomorrow. Lady Cathmore and Lady Hackwell will be there, and I intend to speak to them about a position at Longview."

"You don't wish to leave us?" Mrs. Godwin squeezed the hand she was still holding and smiled. "I confess, I'm glad, but…" She bit her lip.

"My brother's quarrel will be with me, not you. Now, what else needs doing before the service starts?"

THE EARLY ARRIVALS FILTERED INTO THE CHURCH, greeting Eleanor and taking their seats. And just when she thought she might have a reprieve, Matthew walked in with an older gentleman who proved to be Felix Millington.

Where her brother made a show of his austere spirituality, the archdeacon fairly glowed with a kindness she didn't believe was feigned. Shorter than her own tall self, he was portly and jolly and sported a wreathe of white hair like a monk's tonsure. He beamed her a smile and a feeling of peace settled over her.

Or that circle of hair might be an angel's halo.

Mr. Godwin came to join them, and when introductions were made, the archdeacon's large gray eyes twinkled. Even Matthew softened a bit under the man's influence.

And that only lasted until the archdeacon drew Mr. Godwin away to meet Mrs. Godwin.

"You were not at the inn, nor have you moved your things there," Matthew said without preamble.

"No," she said. "I have not."

"What are you about, Eleanor, my dear?" he asked, infusing his tone with a patronizing patience. "I thought that you had abandoned this stubbornness. I've made a place for you in Chichester and even found the possibility of a match for you."

She gasped and laughed. "With that lovely old man? Are you mad?"

His skin mottled a dark shade of red. "Mind your tongue."

"You're being ridiculous, Matthew. I won't marry him. Nor will I be leaving with you in the morning."

Like a big fish seeking to suck in a smaller one, his

lips pursed and then opened again, but before he could speak, the door rattled and the cold air carried in their choir, the children from Longview, with Mrs. McClintock and two of her staff.

"You *will* come with me to the inn tonight," Matthew muttered. "This stubbornness is unbecoming. We will talk after the service."

Despite her determination to go her own way, her confidence was shaken.

"Is anything wrong, my dear?" Mrs. McClintock had taken in the scene, perhaps even heard Matthew's words.

Eleanor forced a smile, shook her head, and turned to the fidgety children. "Now, everyone knows the program?"

The chorus of yeses led to a general hushing, and Eleanor led them to their seats while the rest of the congregation streamed in. With much more fidgeting and arranging and rearranging, the children were finally seated. Christopher Godwin hurried in to join them, and Mr. Godwin appeared from the vestry, garbed and ready. Eleanor ignored her brother beckoning her and squeezed in next to Mrs. McClintock.

As the curate began his welcome, the church door slammed open again with a blast of cold and a late arrival. Mr. Godwin's mouth gaped, and then everyone turned to the shuffling at the door.

Bram was moving up the aisle, a huge bucket of flowers clutched in each arm. Galt followed with more, and behind him came servants.

Glorious white hellebores, Christmas roses, red and white striped carnations, and sprinkled among them vibrant, almost red blooms.

He stopped by her seat. "Sorry I'm late," he said in a stage whisper. "Where do you want these, Eleanor?"

Her breath froze even as heat flooded her cheeks. She tried to speak but her throat had thickened.

"How marvelous, sir." Mrs. Godwin appeared, clapping her hands. She led the men up to the altar.

"We shall have a short delay," Mr. Godwin said, "while we make room among the greenery for this Christmas gift—dare I say Christmas miracle? *The flowers appear on the earth; the time of the singing of birds has come.* In our case it will be the singing of our young children."

Mrs. Godwin directed the placement of the wooden buckets among the urns, putting Eleanor in mind of the earthy shepherds mixed in with the choirs of angels. She looked up to find Bram smiling at her, and an unsettling hope rose in her.

After the carols, the children processed out and returned garbed as the holy family and their entourage of angels and shepherds with a real baby in arms. Eleanor sniffed back a tear and looked around to see many handkerchiefs deployed.

It was *beautiful*, and *touching*, and *memorable*, just as she'd hoped. Whatever the future held for her, she'd have another perfect moment to cling to.

From across the aisle, Matthew scowled at her, and not even that could mar her pleasure.

* * *

THOUGH IT HAD BEEN YEARS SINCE BRAM HAD BEEN IN A church for anything but funerals, the rituals had lodged deep in his soul. Unlike other clerics, Mr. Godwin seemed the real article, a man of God who had the kindness to not bore his congregation to tears with longwinded prayers.

Eleanor was beautiful tonight, a red dress peeping from under her cloak. She looked perfectly content among the restless children, her eyes aglow as much as theirs. While the regiment always managed some holiday merriment in their winter camps, he'd forgotten how magical Christmas could be when reflected in the eyes of children.

The service ended, and Godwin stepped down from the altar into the sea of parishioners. Bram struggled through the crowd to reach Eleanor.

Matthew Gurnwood was making for her also. Oh yes, Bram had felt the good reverend's glare as he'd marched in with flowers for his lady. Bram steeled himself for battle and reached her first.

"Eleanor," he said, and "Oh, Bram," she said at the same time, her voice thick with emotion.

He reached for her hand. "Dear Eleanor, will you—"

"Huxley." With the barest of nods, Gurnwood glared at him before turning back to his sister. "Eleanor, come along with us. The archdeacon and I will escort you to the inn."

A jolly-looking older man had joined their little

group. He looked vaguely familiar, but Bram couldn't say where he'd met the fellow.

Galt stepped up with Millie, a sly look making his lips twitch.

Eleanor cleared her throat and made introductions.

Felix Millington greeted old Galt and Millie and then addressed Bram. "And you sir, I know well, though you probably don't remember me. I was a friend of your late father and mother. Dangled you on my knee before you were breeched. We were all proud to see you grow into such a fine young man. It's well met, we are." He bestowed an amused look on the joined hands. "Do I detect an understanding here?"

"*Oh.*" Eleanor tugged but Bram clamped his other hand over hers.

"I was getting to that, sir." He dropped to one knee. "Eleanor, I've never forgotten you."

"Here now, Huxley," Gurnwood exclaimed. "What do you think—"

"I wrote to you and when you didn't… I assumed… well, I've never forgotten you. Would you make me the happiest of men? Would you marry me?"

Her mouth dropped open.

"You need my approval," Gurnwood sputtered.

Eyes sparkling, her gaze never left Bram's face. "You forget, I'm of age, Matthew."

"I'll vouch for this young man's character, Gurnwood," the archdeacon said. "The only question is, what does your heart say, Miss Gurnwood?"

His whole world was in her dark shiny eyes, his future, his hopes, his dreams.

"I love you, Eleanor."

* * *

WE MUST TALK, HE HAD SAID.

Instead, he was sweeping her away with the suddenness of his proposal and she was being carried away, again.

And yet, and yet... her hand felt right in his. Matthew had whispered pious calumnies against Bram's character, yet everything about Bram felt honorable, and true, and right.

"For pity's sake, Ellie," Galt said, and Millie shushed him.

Eleanor touched his strong jaw and swept her thumb over his cheek. Tenderness flooded her, and desire swept through her again. "I've never forgotten you, either, Bram." She took in a deep breath. She'd prayed for wisdom. And guidance. And an angel to show her the way.

And courage. She'd be stepping out into the unknown.

"Yes," she said, taking a leap of faith. "Yes, Bram, I will marry you."

Bram shot to his feet. Huzzahs sounded around them, and her feet left the ground as he tossed her up into the air.

"Kiss her," someone said.

And he did.

EPILOGUE

One week later

Three clergymen had officiated their wedding that day, the archdeacon himself fetching the license from the bishop in Chichester and insisting on having part of the honor along with a smiling Mr. Godwin and a very subdued Matthew.

Perhaps, under Mr. Millington's influence, her brother would shed some of his pretentiousness.

What with the New Year's Eve celebration and the day's nuptials, the assembly room behind the Royal George Inn had never looked more festive. Nor had Eleanor ever seen such conviviality: farmers, gentry, and the Brockton Manor crowd more or less mingled —less in the case of Lady Felicity and of course, her own brother, Matthew.

After the fine luncheon, Bram accepted congratulations and good wishes, never very far away from her. The weather had turned foul, and the quartet the Viscount hired for dancing sent word that they had to beg off. But an intrepid farmer pulled out a violin, and so there would be dancing.

She hadn't danced with Bram since that long-ago party.

"A waltz," he called.

"I've never waltzed," she whispered.

"It is," he said, waggling his eyebrows, "the next best thing to making love."

She went up on her toes and set her lips to his ears and said, "Why not skip the next best? The bridal suite is ready."

His eyes lit, his lips turned up in a slow smile, and his hand flattened against her back. "Follow my lead, Lady Huxley."

He tucked her close, his touch radiating heat that unfurled within her. The dance floor cleared for the newlyweds, the bow scraped across taut strings, and Bram swept her closer still, his lips hovering, tantalizing and close, as they circled and twirled, and one couple, and then another, and another stepped onto the floor.

Dizzy with the motion, his masculine scent, and sheer desire, she barely noticed when they passed through the doorway and stood in the lamplit passage that led to the inn's reception room. A grinning Alexander Grant closed the door behind them, leaving them alone in the dim light.

Bram pulled her against him, pressed his lips to hers, and then she was floating as he swept her up.

"On to the best thing?" she asked, laughing.

He growled an answer into her ear and took the

45

stairs two at a time, freeing a hand to open and close the bedchamber door, and finally setting her on her feet.

His strong arms came around her, and he raised her chin with one finger, a look of wonder in his eyes.

She took in a breath. "Well?"

The spell broken, he chuckled. "The best thing for tonight. And every night." His thumb swept her lower lip. "But the very best, Eleanor, is knowing I'll have a lifetime with you."

The End

A NOTE FROM THE AUTHOR

I hope you've enjoyed Bram's and Ellie's sweet Christmas romance. If you've read any of my earlier books, you'll recognize some of the players in this story world.

Ellie first appeared in *A Leap Into Love*, a Leap Day romance that tells the story of Alexander Grant and his lady, Maria. Maria, in turn, played a very minor role in *The Marquess and the Midwife*, another holiday romance. And Lords Cathmore and Hackwell were the heroes of *Rosalyn's Ring* and *Courted by the Earl*.

Many thanks go to the Bluestocking Belles, a remarkably supportive group of historical romance authors. I also appreciate the kind readers who've taken the time to send messages and post reviews. Thank you!

To find out more about my books, visit my website, https://alinakfield.com, and sign up for my monthly newsletter.

All the best,
Alina K. Field

ALSO BY ALINA K. FIELD

MARRYING MR. GIBSON

Previously titled *The Bastard's Iberian Bride*

Paulette Heardwyn rushes to visit her dying guardian, set on learning the truth about her father. But the only man with answers takes his secrets to the grave, leaving her penniless—unless she marries his illegitimate son.

https://alinakfield.com/book/marrying-mr-gibson/

THE VISCOUNT'S SEDUCTION

Lady Sirena Hollister has lost everything, even her fey abilities. But when the fairies hand her a chance at a London Season, her schemes for revenge stir up an unknown enemy, and spark danger of a different sort, in the person of a handsome Viscount.

https://alinakfield.com/book/the-viscounts-seduction/

THE ROGUE'S LAST SCANDAL

Falling—literally—into the arms of the *ton*'s most outrageous rogue seems a risky path of escape, but Maria Graciela Kingsley y Romero has no other choice. Only England's greatest spy lord can help her, and he is not to be found—so his son will have to do!

https://alinakfield.com/book/rogues-last-scandal/

THE COUNTERFEIT LADY

Vowing she'll never submit to an arranged marriage, an earl's daughter bolts for the seaside cottage that will someday be hers. But she finds her quiet refuge occupied by the last man she ever wants to see—an American artist, who's also a thief. And quite possibly one of her father's spies.

https://alinakfield.com/book/the-counterfeit-lady/

AVENGING THE EARL'S LADY

The long war is over, but honor requires vanquishing one last enemy, and the Earl of Shaldon has no time for romance. But when the lady he longs for interferes in his plot, and his enemy strikes at her, nothing else matters but avenging his lady.

https://alinakfield.com/book/avenging-the-earls-lady/

NOVELLAS AND HOLIDAY STORIES:

THE MARQUESS AND THE MIDWIFE

Finalist, 2016 National Reader's Choice Award

Uncovering a lie drives a new marquess back from a self-imposed exile at Christmas to find the only woman he's ever loved. Finding her turns out to be easy, uncovering her stunning secrets, a bit harder. But winning her back will be the greatest challenge of all.

https://alinakfield.com/book/the-marquess-and-the-midwife/

A LEAP INTO LOVE

Can a gentleman be too charming?

The ladies of Upper Upton think so.

When the single ladies of the village conspire to teach their charmer a lesson that might bankrupt him, the town's loveliest young widow—who's sworn off marriage forever—steps up to warn him.

https://alinakfield.com/book/a-leap-into-love/

LILIANA'S LETTER

Finalist, 2015 National Reader's Choice Award

The Matchmaker Meets the Matchbreaker

Liliana Ashford's future as a professional chaperone depends on her wealthy charge's successful marriage, but her own close encounter with a scoundrel years ago makes her determined to save the girl from the same kind of rogue.

https://alinakfield.com/book/lilianas-letter/

THE GHOST OF DEPFORD HALL

A sweet Halloween short story

It's her mother's last All Hallows' Eve.

When family, friends, and tenants gather, goblins, ghouls, and ghosts are banned from this All Hallows' Eve party.

Only, no one told the Ghost of Depford Hall!

https://alinakfield.com/book/ghost-depford-hall/

COURTED BY THE EARL

Previously titled *Bella's Band*

A 2015 RONE Award Finalist

Saddled with his brother's title and debts, nothing about this new life makes the Earl of Hackwell want to stay—until he meets a lady with a secret that can change everything.

https://alinakfield.com/book/courted-by-the-earl/

ROSALYN'S RING

2014 Book Buyer's Best Winner, Novella Category

Done with grieving her losses, a late nobleman's daughter has fallen into a tidy spinster's life in London. But when one snowy Christmas Eve, a young woman needs rescue, she seizes the chance to do good—and to recover a family heirloom that ought to be hers.

https://alinakfield.com/book/rosalyns-ring/

HAUNTING MISS FENWICK

Thrilled to finally have a permanent home, a Squire's daughter won't let a supernatural creature scare her away. While hunting the ghost she doesn't believe in, she stumbles upon a mysterious flesh and blood man who might be the key to all of her problems.

https://alinakfield.com/book/haunting-miss-fenwick/

LADY TWISDEN'S PICTURE PERFECT MATCH

Promised York's marriage mart and the hospitality of his cousin's doddering stepmother, Major August Kellborn is shocked to find that his fetching hostess is the one woman who stirs his heart.

https://alinakfield.com/book/lady-twisdens-picture-perfect-match/

FLOWERS FOR HIS LADY

Eleanor Gurnwood has only one goal in sight: to make this year's Christmas service beautiful for the parishioners of St. Tancred's—until the Christmas eve when a man from her past rides in on a white horse.

https://alinakfield.com/book/flowers-for-his-lady/

THE UPSTART CHRISTMAS BRIDES SERIES

THE DUKE SHE DESPISED

Hiding her true identity, a young vicar's widow takes a position as housekeeper in a remote Scottish castle at Christmas for a new duke who years ago sabotaged her chance for happiness. She quickly falls for the duke's charming but not very competent factor, not knowing that he's hiding something also—he's the duke she despised!

https://alinakfield.com/book/the-duke-she-despised/

CONVINCING THE COUNTESS

A penniless widowed countess with trade in her blood descends upon the country manor of her sons' negligent guardian, intent on confronting him about her boys' futures. Instead, she finds his younger brother, a business-minded aristocrat with a penchant for widows and a distaste for emotional entanglements. A man who once witnessed her greatest humiliation. A man offering enticing distractions that threaten to derail all her plans.

https://alinakfield.com/book/convincing-the-countess/

THE IMPETUOUS HEIRESS

Before dashing Lord Loughton can make amends with his neglected fiancée, the lady's meddling cousin delivers her to his doorstep. He soon realizes more is amiss than his carelessness. Can he uncover her secrets and win her back before he loses her altogether?

https://alinakfield.com/book/the-impetuous-heiress/

THE NABOB'S DESIGNING DAUGHTER

Ripped from his prestigious London practice to deliver a Highland duke's heir, a young doctor finds there are more snares awaiting than a risky birth, including a surprise—and worthless—bequest. There's also his best friend's cousin, who's blossomed from mousey to heart-stirringly beautiful, with enough wiles to convince an ambitious man that his heart belongs in the Highlands.

https://alinakfield.com/book/the-nabobs-designing-daughter/

THE MACBETH SERIES

FATED HEARTS

A Love After All Retelling of the Scottish Play

A Scottish Baron returning from two decades at war meets the wife he divorced and the daughter he disavowed before she was born, only to learn that everything he'd believed was a lie. Determined to win back the only woman he's ever loved he must first face the viper who drove them apart.

https://alinakfield.com/book/fated-hearts/

THE COMTESSE OF MIDNIGHT

A Scottish Earl on a quest for the elusive Comtesse de Fontenay, rescues a French lady smuggler during a devastating storm, taking shelter with her. As the stormy night drags on, he suspects she knows the lady he's seeking, the lady who holds the secret to his identity.

https://alinakfield.com/book/the-comtesse-of-midnight/

CLAIMS OF THE HEART

Since a perilous fall, Lucie Macbeth has been seeing more than a settled future as the heiress to a Scottish barony. The visions plaguing her include a man—one far above her class and breeding, and English to boot. He's engaged to a duke's granddaughter as well, and thus wholly inappropriate. Though she can't marry him, and she won't become any man's leman, when the Sight warns her of danger to him, her conscience, and her heart tell her she can't walk away.

https://alinakfield.com/book/claims-of-the-heart/

COMING OCTOBER 10, 2023

UNDER THE HARVEST MOON

A Bluestocking Belles Collection with Friends

As the village of Reabridge in Cheshire prepares for the first Harvest Festival following Waterloo, families are overjoyed to welcome back their loved ones from the war. This collection of nine engaging tales has mysteries, secrets, tensions, reunions, romance, and makes for an unforgettable read.

Includes *Under the Champagne Moon*,

by Alina K. Field.

https://alinakfield.com/book/under-the-harvest-moon/

COMING JUNE 11, 2024

A WALLFLOWER'S MIDSUMMER NIGHT'S CAPER

Book 15 in The Revenge of the Wallflowers multi-author collection.

A Midsummer Night's masquerade at her family's country home presents the Honorable Nancy Lovelace with the perfect opportunity for revenge against the man who ruined her first London season—a man she's known since childhood, a man she once thought she loved.

https://alinakfield.com/book/a-wallflowers-midsummer-nights-caper/